IN THE MOSS

RENARD PRESS — PLAYSCRIPT II

IN THE MOSS: ORIGINALLY PRODUCED BY MRS C'S COLLECTIVE ONLINE IN 2020, DIRECTED BY FRANCESCA GOODRIDGE. NAV PLAYED BY ERIC SHANGO AND JANET PLAYED BY KATHERINE REYNOLDS. FIRST R&D PERFORMANCE AT THE HOPE MILL THEATRE, MANCHESTER IN 2021, DIRECTED BY GEORGI MCKIE. NAV PLAYED BY MUDASSAR DAR AND JANET PLAYED BY SHAREESA VALENTINE.

SPECIAL THANKS TO CHARLOTTE EVEREST, FRANCIS GRIN AND JENNIE EGGLETON AT MRS C'S COLLECTIVE, TO GEORGI MCKIE AND TO MY MUM.

BY THE SAME AUTHOR:

FRIDGE

PLAYSCRIPT I

9781913724238

IN THE MOSS

EMMA ZADOW

RENARD PRESS

RENARD PRESS LTD

Kemp House
152–160 City Road
London EC1V 2NX
United Kingdom
info@renardpress.com
020 8050 2928

www.renardpress.com

In the Moss first published by Renard Press Ltd in 2021

CONTENTS

IN THE MOSS

INSPIRED BY
THE MOSS SIDE RIOTS,
WHICH TOOK PLACE IN MANCHESTER
ON THE 8TH OF JULY, 1981

CHARACTERS

JANET
Twenties, a student nurse.
Mixed race, Manchester accent.

NAV
Twenties, a police constable.
A Sikh, originally from Uganda.
Manchester accent with a slight intonation.

SCENERY
It is not intended that the stage be demarcated into
rooms or inside/outside – there are no walls on stage.

SETTING
The events occur during the night of the 8th of July,
1981, when the Moss Side riots hit Princess Road
and the Moss Side Police Station, Manchester.

PROLOGUE

NAV and JANET exist in their own worlds of the police station and the hospital. Lights, dim and charged, criss-cross over time and space as they put on their uniforms in front of a mirror.

They continue to get dressed while, in the background, there is the sound of an ECG machine thumping, the sound of a window smashing, and the blue flashing lights of police cars criss-cross over them.

NAV: He's crying, screaming.

JANET: He's screaming for his mother.

NAV: He's screaming for his brother.

JANET: He's screaming…

NAV: He's saying, 'Don't let me die. I don't want to die!'
I get information that just bleeps in my ear like an alarm clock that's way too early for your ears but kind of all right for your eyes—

JANET (*to herself*): …and I didn't understand what the other nurse was saying, but I knew that her eyes were telling me to—

NAV: Keep calm!

JANET: Jan, you've never dealt with this much blood in your entire life.

NAV: A boy, tonight, in those riots, because of you.
JANET: Because of me.
NAV: Because of me.
JANET: They always say you're going to kill someone some day.

(*Pause.*)

BOTH: He wasn't meant to be my first.

(*A bell rings. The radio on* NAV*'s belt crackles.*)

RADIO VOICEOVER: All constables report immediately to the station. Repeat. Under attack. Urgent backup required at…
HOSPITAL VOICEOVER: Riot in Princess Road, Moss Side. All medical staff to A&E immediately.

(*There is a faint sound of roaring in the distance. ECG thumps.*)

ACT ONE

Shapes and figures run through the flashing lights. JANET *and* NAV *appear. She rummages for keys to the door in front of them. It's a struggle. He towers over her from behind.* JANET *breathes faster.*

JANET: It's just... normally I'm... I'm more... What always helps is a curry on the way home, a couple of Pils – beers – I'm classy for my age. Two for one at the corner shop. Does me a deal. But that, out there... All those... people.

(*Pause.*)

NAV: Which key is it again, love?

JANET: I don't... don't know.

NAV: Yes, you do. Now. Let's look at the lock. Is it gold or silver?

JANET: Um... I dunno.

NAV: Yes, you do. Answer me.

JANET: Um... gold, I think.

NAV: Now, is it this one?

JANET: No. I'm trying my best. I can't see properly.

NAV: This one?

JANET: Maybe. It's so dark!

NAV: Let's give that a go, shall we? And if not, we'll just
try again.

(*There is an explosion behind them.* NAV *and* JANET *throw themselves through the door. They slam it shut behind them. He leans
his shoulder against it.* JANET *runs to the centre of the room.*)

Get back!

(NAV *looks at her from the door, his shoulder still firm against it.*)

I need you to stay there!

JANET: Why? What have we done?

(*She goes to the middle of the room. The explosions subside. Silence.*)

NAV: I... I need to check the area. Make sure you're
not—

JANET: There's blood on your...

(NAV *opens and slams the door again, hard, locks it and throws
her the key. She catches it. He moves, checking as he goes.*)

Shouldn't we call... I dunno, backup or something?

NAV: Please, just—

JANET: I shouldn't have... I should have been—

NAV: We need to be smart.

(*They jump as another crash sounds;* NAV *grabs* JANET *and pulls them both down on to their stomachs on the floor. Silence. He calculates their next move.*)

JANET: Afraid of a little petrol bomb after the riot shields?

NAV: I didn't exactly see any nurses on the scene.

JANET: What happened out there?

NAV: You got an idea from what was going on in A&E, I'm sure.

JANET (*whispering*): Saalem aleiku… um… aleika-hum, erm… yeah. Oh. Sorry. I'm no good at this.

(NAV *stares at her hard.*)

What? Our Sheila on Hulme Way went with—

NAV: Is there a back door out of here?

JANET: No. Look, I'm sorry. I've already had a shit day, might as well make it a bit unshitter… shittier-less… (*She frowns*).

NAV: Whatever it is, it wasn't your fault.

(*They look at each other.*)

JANET: Thanks.

NAV: These things happen in A&E. I'm sure you did all you could and—

JANET: OK, I get it.

NAV: OK. (*Hurt:*) Glad you got the message. (*Pause.*) Are you sure you're OK?

JANET: I'm fine.
NAV: Get up.

(*They get up slowly, cautiously.*)

JANET: Do you want me to take a look at the wound?
NAV: What?
JANET: The blood. There must be a wound under your
    uniform?
NAV: Oh, no, it's not mine.

(*Slight pause.*)

JANET: Do you mind if I... (*She indicates the next room.*)
    It's just, I'm a bit desperate...
NAV: No, sure. Go for it.
JANET: It's only, do you want to... (*she indicates the bath-
    room again*) check first? That's why you're here, isn't
    it?
NAV: Oh! Right, yeah.

(*He goes into the bathroom and looks around.*)

JANET (*joking*): Anything dangerous in there?
NAV (*from the bathroom*): No. Unless you count me!

(*He returns.*)

JANET: Look, it's not a big flat. It's just me.
NAV: I wanted to. After today. After—

JANET: I'm fine.

NAV: So you keep saying.

JANET: Is this going to take long?

NAV: Listen, there's been reports of nurses being targeted.

JANET: So. You thought you'd be the hero and take me home tonight with no backup. Brilliant. Just brilliant!

(*Pause.*)

NAV: I'm sick of this, this—

JANET: You were there – was it as bad as it seemed from where we were?

NAV: Hot.
On fire.
Fuming cars.
I'd rather—

JANET: Can I get you a drink?

(*Pause.*)

NAV: Are you serious?

(JANET *nods.*)

I think we should stay here. Don't aggravate things with our appearance. I'm not leaving. Not now.

JANET: What about backup? Have you tried the radio or something?

NAV: Faulty. But seeing as I was heading back—
JANET: So we're stuck.
NAV: You got a phone?

(*She laughs.*)

Sh! Shut it, yeah? You got one or not?
JANET: Have *you* got one?
NAV: No.
JANET: Well, then. We're stuck.
NAV: I can't leave until it's safe.

(*There is another crash beyond them. An ambulance siren screeches in and out of earshot.*)

JANET: Talk to me about something.
NAV: Erm… Well…
JANET: Just anything! Please!
NAV: I'm not… good at that stuff.

(*He picks up a small antique china lion from a shelf.*)

JANET: Now!
NAV: All right!

(*Pause.*)

Well, um, d'ya like the Reno, yeah? Well, one at the station said he saw Richard Dunn and Muhammad Ali, right? In the Reno. Ali. '76. Right there in front of him. Right after they were like… (*He enacts a left hook and double jab.*)

JANET: Watch it! That's… very delicate.

NAV: Sorry.

(*He gives it back to her.*)

JANET: It was… from a school trip.

NAV: What weird trips did your school do?

JANET: I pretend he lets out a little roar every time I walk past him.

NAV: Bit weird, that.

JANET: Maybe it helps when I'm scared.

(*She walks past him to the bathroom. She makes a roar sound.*)

NAV: It's strange, because in the hospital you seemed like a normal girl. But you're completely mad, aren't you?

JANET (*swiping it from him*): It was a school trip to the zoo!

NAV: Everything in miniature unnerves me.

JANET: I love lions.

NAV: Leo, are we?

JANET: No.

NAV: Horoscope?

JANET: Fuck off.

NAV: I just thought you'd be into all of that sun–moon stuff.

JANET: Um, it was years ago. Mrs Fletcher brought it back for me. She must've thought I'd like a lion.

Dad said it was a waste of time. His money could go towards more important things. Lions don't get visits from girls like me. Miss said I didn't miss much. But I got bullied cos of the whole zoo thing.

(*Pause.*)

Do you think lions have accents? Like you and me?

(NAV *stares at her in astonishment.*)

Like, if one from, I dunno, San Diego, met one from, say, Salford – that's where me cousins are from – they'd understand each other?

NAV: Tonight is going to go really fast or really slow.

(*Sirens moan outside.*)

I reckon it would be more a factor whether they were born in said zoo in question or in the wild.

JANET: Good point.

NAV: He isn't called Parsley, is he?

JANET: No, Sage. (*Pause, then, trying to make a joke, and coming off completely over the top:*) Because I'm a bloody anarchist!

(*He doesn't smile, and fidgets uncomfortably.*)

Sorry. That was terrible. You're not going arrest me, are you?

(*They smile. She looks down at his uniform jacket. He looks at the sleeve of her scrubs.*)

BOTH: There's... on your...
JANET: Here, let me—
NAV: No! I mean, I wouldn't want to put you out.
JANET: It's the same...

(*He starts to take his jacket off.*)

NAV: Where do you normally...

(*He pats his jacket and drapes it over his arm.*)

Do you have a bowl?
JANET: Yeah. I need to get out of this thing.
NAV: I'll wait at the door.

(*They move towards the bedroom.* JANET *paces back and forth, nervous, uncertain, and picks some clothes, then changes her mind, then changes it again.*)

Just for one night. One night, OK?

(*He hits his head against the wall.*)

(*Trying to hold it together:*) You OK in there?
JANET (*picking a third jumper*): Yeah, yeah, just had my
    first, but apart from that, I'm great, petal!

(*He puts his head in his hands. He loosens his top button.*)

NAV: First time for everything, eh?

(*He picks up the radio and turns it on quietly.*)

RADIO VOICEOVER: Gupta? Gupta?

(*He turns it off. It whines out of tune to a crackle.*)

JANET: You got anyone waiting on you?
NAV: Funny. Very funny.
JANET: I dunno, anyone. Fetch the toothpaste, would ya?
NAV (*struggling*): I'm sure I won't need to stay the night.
JANET: For the blood!

(*He looks down at his jacket. He jumps upright, fast and rigidly. He's on duty again. He knocks on the door. She opens it and appears, now dressed in her own clothes.*)

Toothpaste?
NAV: What?
JANET: Toothpaste!

(*He stares at her, thrown by seeing her out of uniform. She walks past him and into the bathroom.*)

There's a basin. Could you fetch it and fill it?
NAV: Uhuh.

(*He busies himself finding it.*)

JANET: Cold water, mind!

(*She returns with the toothpaste and a cloth.*)

NAV: Uhuh.

(JANET *continues moving around while* NAV *tries to fill the basin with water.*)

JANET: It felt like seeing fleets of hearses, when the Black Mariahs went past.
NAV: When *we* came, you mean? Our vans?

(*Pause.*)

It's never the nurse's fault. Sorry.
JANET: I've never seen so many horses before. And they kept coming, y'know? They just kept coming. Never known horses like that in Moss Side. Never.

(*Pause.*)

NAV: There was blood… and when it dried…
JANET: Like crushed candy floss at Blackpool.
NAV: Like my sister's wedding day, all pink and gold.
JANET: And it starts to peel off my hands as I rub them together from the cold.

(*She runs her fingers through her hair. Shapes distort in the shadows, showing the riots. Her hands shake. She takes a cigarette out, and a lighter. She keeps flicking it, getting more and more agitated.* NAV *looks at her fingers.*)

NAV: You want a… light, love?

(*A siren rattles past them. She struggles with the lighter. He takes it, shakes it up and down and finally gets it lit for her. She inhales deeply.*)

JANET: Is this a sick, twisted attempt at small talk?
NAV: S'pose.
JANET: Did you do the usual?
NAV: Usual?
JANET: Questions.
NAV: Oh.
JANET: You know, the question question questions?
NAV: The 'Stay with Me' questions? Um…
JANET: What's your name? How old are you? What year is it? Who's Prime Minister? What's your favourite colour? What's your mother's name? What's your favourite place? What's the last thing you did you regret? What's the first thing you did you're sorry for?
NAV: If you could be anywhere right now, where would you be?
JANET: What are you doing next year? Anyone waiting for you at home? They'll miss you. That stuff. Yeah.

(*He turns around. There is more shouting in the background.*)

NAV (*changing the subject*): How long you been living here?

JANET: Three years. It was my aunt's. She left it to me.

NAV: Lucky you. What did she do to get this?

JANET: She was the white aunt.

NAV: Sure.

JANET: I'm not myself tonight.

NAV: Yeah. What's your dad do?

JANET: Tailor.

(*She stubs out her cigarette.*)

NAV: Don't you have an ashtray or something?

(JANET *nods and laughs at him.* NAV *finds one and brings it to her.*)

Well, if the mountain won't come to whatever.

JANET: I'm not after anything tonight!

NAV: No. I know. I'm just trying—

JANET: To help?

(*Silence.*)

NAV: Look, just cos you lost one tonight, it doesn't mean you didn't do a good job.

JANET: Uhuh. Just one boy… Sorry. Never mind.

NAV: Won't last for ever, love. None of us have the energy for this to keep happening.

JANET: That's what they tell us on the TV and the radio and the papers. So it must be true, right?

(*Slight pause.*)

NAV (*overcompensating*): Guilty! Look, um, I'm…

(*They stare at each other some time before breaking the silence.*)

There's something I need to…

(*He sets the basin in front of them. They kneel.* JANET *gestures at his jacket. He puts it in the basin sheepishly. She puts her scrubs in with the jacket. She swirls them together in the basin. She takes his jacket and he takes her scrubs.*)

JANET (*holding the toothpaste*): You see? Pea size. Straight on it. Like that. See?

(*She hands him the toothpaste tube. He does the same. She then scrubs with her fingers. He follows her lead, clearly uncertain what to do with laundry. There is silence. Water swirls and swashes. She scrubs hard.*)

There's a lot, isn't there? Blood, I mean.
NAV: It's been a long night.
JANET: And it's not even finished, is it?
NAV: Janet?
JANET: Yeah?

(NAV *looks at her.*)

NAV: Nothing.

JANET: How many brothers you got?

NAV: None.

JANET: Sisters?

NAV: Two.

JANET: Uh oh. I'm from here, by the way – well, sort of, but anyway, yeah.

NAV: Uganda, me.

(*He joins her. The following should be fast.*)

JANET: Heck. Thought you were going to say Bradford then. But well, wow. Did you always want to be a—?

NAV: No.

JANET: Okaaaay…

NAV: I wasn't meant to be there.

JANET: What, Bradford?

NAV: Be real. No. In the riot.

JANET: Thought… well… OK, then. Be careful with mine! That's cotton and viscose. I'm not having it shrink on me again! Bloody sizing is all over the place.

NAV: All over the place. Yeah. That's me.

JANET: You don't look like you're from—

NAV: Oh God. Don't say that. Oh, OK, fine. But don't say that.

JANET: You can ask me too! If you fancy.

NAV: One day we're at home, and the next, Dad says Amin has given us just days to get out. Days. And that was it. We left. With nothing but each other. Or… you know.

JANET: Sure.

(*Pause.*)

I'm shit at caring about people. I thought you
should know that.
NAV: Yeah, you really don't need to share that with me.
JANET: I'm the over-sharer type. Always have been. Let
me know if it starts annoying you.
NAV: I will.

(*They stare at each other.*)

JANET: Why do you always feel just a little bit less scared
when there's two of you scared together?
NAV: Yeah, but why does it have to happen here? In the
Moss?

(*Pause.*)

What if…
JANET: Is he——
NAV: And I'm a——
JANET: What would that make me? You know?
BOTH: He was my first and I can't even——
JANET: You're a flaming nurse. You're surrounded by
death every day, and you're going to be for a very,
very long time. You can't be like this.

(*They both catch a strange scent and smell themselves.*)

BOTH: I smell of blood.

NAV: I need a shower.

JANET: I need a Valium.

BOTH: Pull yourself together!

NAV: You just need to hold it together a little while longer.

JANET: I know.

NAV: I was talking to myself.

(*The radio crackles again from his belt. He picks it up.*)

RADIO VOICEOVER: WHAT IS GOING ON, GUPTA? IT'LL BE GOING ON YOUR REPORT IF ANYTHING HAPPENS TO THAT NURSE!

(*He turns the volume down frantically and ignores it.*)

JANET: Maybe I should change. I'm really sticky.

(*He wipes himself down. She's terrified. He's blank. She inhales. He inhales. She continues to clean ferociously. He tries to concentrate. There is an awkward silence between them.*)

NAV: There's a story we were told, back in Uganda. Before I'd even heard of a place called Moss Side. And Manchester. And everything here.

(*She doesn't look up. During the following, she cleans faster and faster.*)

So one day, in a village outside of Darjeeling which no one can find, there was a Brahmin, a holy man, who passed a tiger in a trap. The tiger pled for his release, promising not to eat the Brahmin. 'Let me out of this cage, oh kind one!' cried the tiger. The man, see, sets the tiger free out of pity, but no sooner is the tiger out of the cage than he says he is going to eat the man after all. The man is horrified, outraged, and tells the tiger just how unjust he is; so they agree to resolve the issue by asking the judgement of the first three things they encounter. The first thing they meet is a tree, who has suffered greatly at the hands of humans, and answers that the tiger should eat the Brahmin. Next, they come across a buffalo, who has been exploited and mistreated by humans, and agrees it is fair and just that the Brahmin should be eaten. Next, they meet a jackal, who is more sympathetic towards the man. Feigning ignorance, he asks the tiger to show him the trap. When he is taken to it, he still claims not to understand, so the tiger gets in to demonstrate – at which moment the jackal leaps over and shuts him in. He tells the man that he should never see the tiger again, and he should forget all about the incident. (*Pause.*) Janet? Hello?

JANET: It's the same blood on us both, isn't it, when you think about it?

(*A siren goes past.*)

NAV: Well, I—
JANET: So, the tiger just gets tricked back into the cage?
NAV: I—
JANET: What's the point in that?

(NAV *scrubs a bit harder.*)

I think the jackal should eat the man instead.
NAV: What?
JANET: The riot.
NAV: Yeah?
JANET: How many tigers were with you?
NAV: I guess there were—
JANET: More than you.

(*Pause.*)

NAV (*looking down at the clothes*): It's not your fault.

(*She scrubs harder. He tries to catch up with her.*)

JANET (*smirking*): It's never the nurse's fault, remember?
NAV: It wasn't, though.

(*She scrubs harder.*)

JANET: I know.
NAV: No, you really—
JANET (*snapping*): Here's a story for you. Once upon a
    time, a girl was born in Manchester. Her daddy was

born somewhere else. But Manchester broke him apart. Into so many pieces – they were scattered so far. And all she wanted was to put him back together. And she couldn't find all the pieces of him to make him better again. So he went to go find those pieces for her. And her mum still loved her. And wanted her to grow up and do the things she couldn't do. So she did. Her best to, anyway.

(NAV *looks at her, concerned. She reacts with a shrug.*)

Blah blah blah. The bloody end! How's that for a flaming fairy tale for you? No tigers, no princes, no nothing. I'm still here. I'm still here!

NAV: So am I.

JANET: Ow!

NAV: What?

JANET: Your button. It scratched me!

NAV: Mine? You mean yours!

JANET: It was yours, and ow, that really hurt!

NAV: You shouldn't have been—

JANET: I have plasters in the bathroom.

NAV: I'll get one.

(*He leaves for the bathroom.* JANET *is left with the uniform jacket and basin. The water is tinged a sludgy crimson.*)

Where are they?

(*She plunges her hand in the basin of water.*)

JANET (*to herself*): It was your fault. Your fault. Get over it, stupid girl. Come on, stupid bitch, not with a police constable! (*To* NAV*:*) Bottom shelf!

(*She rises quickly and clears the basin to the side and hangs the scrubs and jacket on the back of two chairs. They hang, dripping a little, throughout the scene.*)

NAV: None left!

JANET: Oh well. Not that bad if you look at it, see? Fancy a drink?

NAV: I can't. I'm on duty.

JANET: I'm not. You ever been on a night out with a group of student nurses? Wow, that's messy!

NAV: No.

JANET: Shame.

NAV: Seen 'em, though. You *lot* can put them away.

JANET: Sure can, Constable!

NAV: Don't say it like that.

JANET: Like what?

NAV: Like *that*.

JANET: Yes, *sir*!

NAV: Constable Gupta.

JANET: Do you do this often?

(*She chuckles sarcastically. He doesn't.*)

NAV: Maybe we should just get through this as professionally as we can.

JANET: Yes, sir. I mean, Constable.

NAV: Well, someone's got to be professional in all of this. Someone has got to stop it.

JANET: We tried that all ready tonight.

NAV: Just have to wait it out.

JANET: A drink would be nice. Helps you to forget.

NAV: Maybe we should remember, all right?

JANET: What's worth remembering about 1981?

(*Pause.*)

NAV: You're a good person, Janet.

JANET: Fuck off.

(*They laugh.*)

I messed up. I can't keep making mistakes any more. All I've ever done is fuck up stuff. And I get the one job where if you make a mistake, people die. PEOPLE. DIE.

NAV: You're a good person, I can tell. You have pink hair.

JANET: Could you stop being so bloody nice? I need you to be the pig you are. I want a policeman in *here* to take me out *there*.

NAV: We don't arrest people for doing their job.

JANET: But I killed someone tonight. I did. *I* did. Me. And you should do something about that. I'm sick, sick, *sick* of being told I'm a good person. You know, they laugh at us behind our backs. Trying to make a difference, and I'm only making it worse. I shouldn't care. I shouldn't!

NAV: I don't believe you.

JANET: I didn't give a toss about making a difference.

(*Pause.*)

NAV: Maybe we should have some tea…

JANET: Don't go through my cupboards!

NAV: Bit of vodka, maybe? (*Trying to distract her.*) A dribble of something that resembles shandy? Well, *someone's* classier than they seem.

JANET: I can't do this any more.

NAV: Oh, now.

JANET: What? You always dreamt of being a little PC Plod doing the rounds, with your little hat and little baton, whistling down the road?

NAV: This is the stress talking.

JANET: Stop talking to me like we're friends.

NAV: Would you rather a prison guard?

JANET: You can't keep me here.

NAV: And I'm protecting Moss Side.

JANET: From what? What if it's you, not me, they're throwing shit at?

NAV: We can't be sure, but we need to stay here. And, by the way, your bedside manner must be really, really outstanding.

JANET: I just want to keep going,
Going…
Going…
Going…
Until it can…

NAV: Stop.
    Stop it.

(*They move and begin making the tea together during the following; only the mugs should be real.* JANET *makes a little roar as she passes the ornamental lion.*)

JANET: I was *trained* to care. I'm in the corner. Doctors do the mains. They drive home to the detached and the dog. We're not paid enough to take too much time. I lost that boy today.

NAV: If you really didn't care, you'd have forgotten about Ryan. But you haven't. Let's get that tea going.

(*Pause.*)

JANET: Ryan? That was his name, yeah.

(*Pause.*)

    I just completely and royally fucked up. When we do something right, it's like we don't exist, but when we do something wrong, the whole world comes crashing in on us and it's all our fault.

NAV: Um, any sugar?

JANET: Shit. Tea. Right. No. I've only got what's left. Haven't had time for the shop this week. Do you like it black?

NAV: Black is fine.

JANET: Thank God.

(*Pause.*)

I just feel like everything's going wrong.

(NAV *is silent.*)

What was I—
NAV: You were royally messing up.
JANET: Yeah! All that… I dunno, um… blood… all that
noise in there? With that stupid paper toilet cover
on my head! I just couldn't hear myself think!

(*She goes to get some pink wafers.*)

I mean, if you can't think, what can you do?

(*He sips during the following.*)

(*She sips.*) And I could see the disappointment…

(*He takes a pink wafer and dunks it in his tea.*)

…in Matron's eyes. Like, Why have I wasted my time
with this one? I knew she'd be trouble. I knew she'd
the 'problem case' this year. She's just like all of them
from homes like that. Broken in the head, that girl.

(NAV *looks down into his tea.*)

NAV: Oh no.

JANET: What?

NAV: I lost my pink wafer. Well, half of it.

JANET: Oh, I'm so sorry.

(NAV *throws the remaining half into his mouth and starts trying to fish the lost half out of the tea. He struggles to do this during the following.*)

I was supposed to be better than they thought I was, blood under my nails, bags under my eyes, pounding my rhythm by focusing on the lyrics to 'Another One Bites the Dust'.

(NAV *sips a bit more of the tea, which still has half a wafer in it.*)

NAV: I thought you nurses used that idiotic little elephant, Nelly the—

JANET: The Elephant. Yeah. (*Sings half-heartedly.*)

(NAV *rolls his eyes, increasingly annoyed.*)

NAV: And, you just had to sing it, didn't you?

JANET: So, I came up with using 'Another One Bites the Dust' instead.

NAV: What, Queen?!

JANET: Shut up!

NAV: No judgement here. You do you.

JANET: But I couldn't do it. Something inside me stopped working. Cos it goes into that bit, doesn't it? That… (*Badly, slightly embarrassed:*) …You can beat him, you can cheat him… you can—

(NAV *has found the wafer at the bottom of the tea.*)

NAV: —treat him bad.

(*They smirk together. He doesn't know where to put the wafer.*)

JANET: I looked down and there was nothing. I saw the dirt under my nails, and I thought, No one deserves to have me here. I'm—
NAV: Gone…

(*He shows her the mug, which evidently contains a mess of dissolved biscuit.*)

JANET: That's disgusting. You've made a mess of that.
NAV: Sorry. I didn't mean to.
JANET: I know.
NAV: I'm really, really sorry. Janet, I…

(*Pause.*)

JANET: How's that jacket coming on?

(*She goes to where the jacket and scrubs are hanging. She freezes.*)

(*In a sing-song voice:*) It's not quite ready!

(*He looks at his jacket. He runs over to it.*)

NAV: What have you done to my uniform?!
JANET: I cleaned it!
NAV: You've bleached it!
JANET: It's just toothpaste!
NAV: What am I going to do when I walk in tomorrow?
JANET: Nothing, because nothing is wrong with it.
NAV: Look at it! It's all white!
JANET: That's what happens!
NAV: I can't believe you.
JANET: Nav, it's just a uniform.
NAV: It's not just a uniform!

(*Pause.*)

What are they going to say at the station? I'm already the outsider. What's Serge going to say?

(*He recovers quickly, controlling his temper.*)

JANET: All right! (*After glancing at him, she says, in the voice of the Serge, exaggerated:*) You're under my roof, son. My rules.
NAV: What?
JANET: You heard me.
NAV: Janet, I'm not——

(JANET *grabs his constable's jacket and swings it over her shoulders. It drowns her, but it looks rather good on her.* NAV *looks at her.*)

What are you doing?

JANET: What does it look like?

NAV: There are many things I could say.

JANET: I'm him! The Serge!

NAV: Well, I wasn't thinking that.

JANET (*impersonating the Serge again*): That's not how to talk to a superior constable, Gupta!

NAV: This isn't funny.

(JANET *walks up to him confrontationally, still in the style of the Serge.*)

JANET: Was that a question? I'll just have to make a terrible joke at your expense in order to feed my enormous… ego! Ha ha ha.

NAV: This really isn't as funny as you think it is.

JANET: Really, Constable? I thought better of you. And what's this? A stain?

NAV: From a nurse, last night.

(JANET *raises her eyebrow.*)

Oh, grow up, will ya?

JANET: This is still a stain. A stain. We can't have that. Not in my unit. I won't stand for it. And stains are mistakes. Stains are signs of sloppiness, inadequacy and…

NAV: That's enough! I know what they'll say. You don't need to…

JANET: So what are you going to say to them, then?

NAV (*smiling venomously*): Thank you, sir. For your…
observation. I will do better next time.

(*Pause. She shifts.*)

JANET: Where are you going?

NAV: Oh, it's not over. This thing you think is so funny.

JANET: Don't take that tone with me.

NAV: I see what you're doing.

JANET: I've decided to stop and search you, due to the
stain on your blazer. I won't have it. I've not stopped
you because of any other reason. I'm a modern
man, see. The sus law states I can stop or arrest you
if I suspect you of loitering with intent to commit
an arrestable offence.

NAV: All right. Enough.

JANET: I don't care if you've had enough. We've all had
enough! Enough of you. I don't care if your mum
sent you to the corner shop for milk. I don't care if
you're on your way to Alexandra Park, school or the
dentist. I'm going to stop you. Because I want to.
Because I can. I'm going to arrest you if you refuse.
Y'hear? Only way to teach you lot to never have a
stain again.

NAV: OK, I get it!

(*Pause.*)

JANET (*still in the voice of the Serge, but sounding more genuine*):
Gupta. What I meant to say was… you're… doing

a fine job. And any constable in this station would be lucky to have you as their partner. You're… doing us proud, son. Constable, it's an honour to have you. Now, get back to work before we make the others jealous.

(NAV *looks at her.*)

(*As herself again:*) Don't look at me like that.
NAV: Like what?
JANET: Like I just told you I had a boyfriend.

(*Pause.*)

You know what they do. They stop boys. In the Moss. I've seen how they do it. Walking to school. Then they're late. Again and again and again. In the Moss. Then their mum gets a call. Then sometimes they stop going to school altogether. Then the sus laws come on them hard. In the Moss. On suspicion of… well, whatever they want. Some boys get arrested for standing with their friends. Playing kerby. No one sees them for a bit. They come back with a bruise, a broken something. Have you seen the graffiti on Claremont Road? 'Help the police, beat yourself up.' Classic.

(*A light flashes across the stage again.*)

We're all a bit fucking fed up with it now. Y'know?

(*A large smash is heard, slightly further away than last time. They freeze.*)

NAV: Give me that!

(*He rips the jacket off her.*)

JANET: Jesus! Ow!

NAV: You should keep your voice down. Stop messing around.

JANET: Afraid of everyone outside, are we?

NAV: No. I just think under the circumstances—

JANET: Oh! I'm sorry. Sh! We should all be quiet and just let this 'blow over'.

NAV: We may be being watched. Policeman goes into a nurse's flat and...

JANET: Sounds like a joke – a bad dad joke! What's the punchline?

(*A smash is heard.*)

NAV: That's enough.

(*He ducks low. He drags her down with him.*)

JANET: Not the drink we had planned, is it?

NAV: You planned! And shut up.

JANET: Where are our manners now?

NAV: Shut up! (*A bubble of rage seethes inside him.*) You care too much.

JANET: Is that a thing where you're from?

NAV: No. It's a Manc thing.

(*She laughs. He covers her mouth with his hand, then moves to the door to check outside.*)

JANET: Why was Ryan so special to you? What were you going to tell me before?

NAV: Nothing. He was in cookery school is all. Second year. Anyway. You cared too.

(*Pause.* JANET *looks hard at* NAV.)

JANET: Yeah, but I've got maternal instinct as an excuse to fall back on. But you?

NAV: Human beings like picking sides. We can't help ourselves. It comes all too naturally.

JANET: Do you think someone some day will thank us? For all of this?

NAV: I dunno. If I wanted eggs thrown at me, I'd have stayed in Pap's shop.

JANET: Munchies and shoplifters. Maybe not.

NAV: Not that I can't now.

BOTH (*quoting parents*): You've been given an opportunity by this country to make a difference. You better take it.

NAV (*impersonating his father*): I didn't bring you over here for you to become waster boy hanging out on the streets. We came here from Uganda.

JANET: My dad was from Jamaica. Sometimes I remember him looking at me as if I was a free prize in his cereal.

NAV: Don't ask me if I miss it.

JANET: What, Uganda?

NAV: It was over ten years ago now. This is where I am now. And I'm going to take care of it.

(*His radio crackles and makes him jump.* JANET *lights up and smokes. He goes to the door to check again. He turns the main lights off and shadows leap and morph around them. An ambulance goes past. An ECG machine thumps, low and slow.*)

It's not gonna be like this for ever.

JANET: I don't know if I want to be around to see what happens next.

NAV: What's left will be ours.

JANET: I know I'm not the easiest to be stuck with, but can we try to be—

(*The radio crackles again, louder, sounding throughout the room like a deathly cough.*)

RADIO VOICEOVER: Station under strain. It's not over. Gupta. Urgent need…

(NAV *grabs it and rushes to the door. He leans against it again. He switches back to the police station radio out of desperation. He checks quickly, efficiently.*)

JANET: Is that dead?!

(NAV *does not answer.*)

Is that radio dead?!

(*He returns to her. He smacks the radio hard to try and jolt it.*)

We're alone, aren't we?

NAV: I think we need to be calm.

JANET: Don't you tell me to be calm!

NAV: I didn't mean for this to happen!

JANET: Oh, we never bloody do, do we?!

NAV: Shut it. I need to think! Let me think!

JANET: Are you even a real policeman?

NAV: I don't see you coming up with any ideas, you
    stupid girl!

(JANET *turns him around firmly.*)

JANET: Whose blood was it on your uniform? Why
    can't you say?

NAV: Will. You. Stop.

(*Pause.*)

JANET: OK. Fine. You do not get to tell me what to do!
    Whose blood was it?

(*He goes towards her with force, but stops himself and throws
the radio across the space. There is a bright light outside and
a crash.* JANET *doesn't move.* NAV *retreats out of shame
to the corner. He crosses his arms. Silence. They look over
at each other intermittently, missing each other's gaze. Sirens*

go past in the distance. Red and blue lights in morphed shapes cascade over the carpet as an ambulance drives past. Its screams are warped by the Doppler effect, as though in and out of focus.)

Have you felt like that before?

(*Pause.*)

NAV: Have you?

JANET: Yep. Like you just want to hit, punch, something… anything… until you see what you're feeling go away?

(NAV *is silent.*)

Yeah, me too.

(*Pause.*)

NAV: I'm not a bad person.

JANET: None of us are.

NAV: Your dad tell you that?

(*Pause.*)

JANET: I'm not stupid. Please don't call me what everyone else does. I didn't do things because I believed that for so long. So… yeah. Just, I'm not stupid, all right? Please.

NAV: I'm sorry.

(*She picks up his uniform jacket and inspects it.*)

JANET: Nav?
NAV: Oh my God, what now?
JANET: How did you know Ryan was in cookery school?
 Did you know him?

(*They watch each other.*)

NAV: No, I didn't.
JANET: Yes you did.

ACT TWO

Continuous.

NAV (*changing the subject*): I… You should know… I turned
the radio off. I switched it away from the police
bandwidth earlier.

JANET: YOU DID WHAT?!

NAV: I didn't think it was a big problem. I just wanted
to—

JANET: Fuck the nurse? Brag to the boys at the station?
Play the hero after saving us all from the big bad
rioters tonight?

NAV: I know it looks bad. But I put it back on. It must
have lost the signal in switching back. Janet, I don't
know why I did it, OK? I fucked up. I fucked up.

JANET: You're too right you have, you lying prat! I
almost felt sorry for you then.

NAV: I saw you outside the hospital tonight and I didn't
want you to be alone. After Ryan, after… tonight.
Can't you see how I wouldn't want you to be alone?

JANET: You mean, you didn't want to be alone.

NAV: Neither of us did.

JANET: But, why the radio?

NAV: I panicked.

JANET: This isn't some little boy's game we're playing, tuning the radio in and out! People are being shot at out there! In my street! My city! My city is burning and there's nothing I can do about it!

NAV: I was there! You don't have to tell me how a car burns and how it smells… like burning hair… but I suppose you wouldn't know about that, would you?

JANET: I killed someone tonight; do you have any idea what that feels like?!

NAV: Yes!

(*Pause.*)

We all get the same speech in training. You'll kill someone eventually. That first was today. That's all. And I thought, in a crazy way, that made us tied somehow. That we have something to share. And I didn't want anyone else getting in the way of that; I didn't want to be alone on a night like that. And neither did you.

(JANET *gives him a good hard look. She slowly walks over to the radio. He doesn't stop her. She flicks it on. Slowly. Calmly.*)

JANET: Hello?

(*Pause.*)

Hello?

(*It crackles. It hurts their ears.*)

It just keeps doing that wavering thing.

(NAV *nods.*)

Just when you made me feel safe, too. (*She puts a stray hair behind her ear.*) This isn't happening. This isn't happening.

(*She begins to hyperventilate.* NAV *tries to distract her.*)

NAV: What's that in your hair?
JANET: Huh?
NAV: That pink?
JANET: It's hot pink.
NAV: What makes it hot?
JANET: I dunno, do I?! I'm not sure if hot pink is really me any more.
NAV: I like it.
JANET: Really? It was going tomorrow.
NAV: Sleep on it. What else could you be? I can't picture you any other way.

(*Pause.*)

I'm not supposed to cut mine.
JANET: You what?
NAV: I'm not meant to, you know, cut it.
JANET: What, at all? Why?

NAV: I told you, Sikh.

JANET: Oh.

(*Pause.*)

Is that the one with the turbans?

NAV: Yes. It's the one with the turbans. But I have to cut it cos of all of this, the duty – people don't like a policeman with long hair.

JANET: Oh, is that why you've been banned from wearing a turban? Because of joining the police?

NAV: No! And I've not been banned!

JANET: Then why don't you wear one?

NAV: Because I cut my hair.

JANET: So, you were kicked out of Sikh Club?

NAV: It's not a club. And no.

JANET: Bit like God Squad?

NAV: No. And you can't say that.

JANET: Which one?

NAV: Neither!

JANET: Why do you cut your hair, then?

NAV: Because I need to not look like me, don't I! Just for a moment, my favourite time of day is first thing in the morning. Before I get up and walk to the bathroom. Before I look in the mirror and I'm me. I'm not my dad.

I'm British.

(*Pause.*)

JANET: When I cut my hair, I felt so cool – it was the last thing my family expected.

(*Pause. He smirks. She nudges him. He nudges her back.*)

Sorry. You're no one else but Nav to me. I've not really been anywhere, me, and I say things I don't understand. I've not really done anything at all, ever. My family's never been anywhere. Done anything. Maybe that's why I'm trying to be a nurse. To do something for someone else.

(*Pause.*)

NAV: I got into this because I wanted someone like me to answer the call the next time my parents' shop was smashed in. To turn up at the door and listen to them.

(*Pause.*)

First thing Pap does here is set up shop. He had one in Uganda – a big one, took care of business for most of the neighbourhood. But… we started from scratch here all over again. He was clever when he got here. G & Sons. He only had one son, but always promised he'd have more. Papaji stays behind one night late. Mum's not happy about this cos she's cooked his favourite. Gulab jamuns. Sweet and sticky. If she didn't, we'd never hear the bloody end of it for weeks. He'd go on about how last year's didn't happen. There was no rose water sugar in his beard. No saffron in the kitchen. 'No culture in this country.' You can have culture without Gulab jamuns, Pap! 'The mother is the first teacher in all of life! We respect her when she feeds!' I want to call him Dad, like you, but Papaji is what he wants. Papaji's thing, that was. One of the last things they brought over from their home when they were making ours. We brought a piece of us here. Pans spitting out pistachios at us. Burnt green. And Mamaji's gold spoons are on the table. They're the size of two fat frogs sitting at the pond. She was actually from India. Before. So, when they come out, you know it's supposed to be special. The frosted sugar scuffs on the table corner. We're thinking, Bit odd that. He'd never miss this. And if he did, we'd be blamed for it! Turns out, he's stayed back to count the change. The change! So stubborn. Dads are like that, aren't they? Just have to know exactly where they are before they leave anywhere. He couldn't leave the shop until he had counted all the petty cash. So he can leave knowing whether he made a profit or not. Gives him pride, that. Understandable. Every day. But today, Mrs McKenzie decided to loaf off about her sister-in-law, so Dad got cornered by her 'You know what ah mean?'s and didn't get a chance to count like he normally does. Finally, after some free gum, she leaves. So he's counting. He's doing his job. And Gulab jamuns are waiting for him. Just like *his* mamaji did a long time ago. Before Uganda. Before me and my sisters. And…

(*Pause.*)

He sees them outside. 'Bloody boys,' he thinks. It's not the first time. And rose water in his beard. Gulab jamuns waiting for him. He's nearly counted it all. He smiles. A profit today. And…

(*Pause.*)

Something hard shatters our window. It shatters over Pap. He's on his knees. Hands. Overhead. Counter's now a barricade, like an overturned car. Everything feels big and small at the same time. He pants. It's over in a second. He peels his hands from his head and it's sticky. Hot. Shop phone. 'Boys will be boys, Mr Gupta,' Police say. It's only then that he realises he can't see some of the shop. It's dark. Darker than before. It's hot, sticky, like home, like where he wants to be… And there's Gulab jamuns waiting for him. Like how his mamaji made them.

(*Pause.*)

Half blind now.

(*Pause.*)

Why can't I be like everybody else?

(JANET *moves towards him.*)

JANET: I've never been to India.

(*Pause.*)

NAV: Neither have I.

(*Pause.*)

JANET: I've been to Blackpool, though. Have you?
NAV: Yeah. It's pretty good. Ice cream in winter and all
    that.
JANET: Smashing, ain't it?
NAV: Yeah, great, that tower – and the rides!

(*They gently laugh and move closer together. They look at each
other.*)

JANET: Nav, what happened to you?

(NAV *is silent. He moves away from her.*)

I need you to tell me the truth. Should I be afraid
of you?

(*Long pause.*)

NAV: I don't want you to be.
JANET: But should I be?

(*Pause. A loud crash outside makes them duck down together. Sirens. A light bulb bursts, making it a bit darker than before. They cascade to the floor once more. The crash and bulb smash has triggered something within them. They separate from each other and shapes distort around them.*)

NAV: I want to be honest with you.
JANET: So do I.

(*During the following,* NAV *and* JANET *act out their own memories, whilst also acknowledging each other, checking in with one another. The ECG machine thumps louder.*)

I was tending a wound on one of the patients down in Ward C. Basic stuff – you know, minor head injury. Round the face.
NAV: I was warned. That this is going to be serious. It was the station. We're under attack. It's spread. It's bad.
JANET: I was warned that it's gonna be something I've not dealt with. Big wheels charring, scrambling, scratching, wheeling. Wheel. Bed. Right. Corner goes over my foot twice. Left and Right.
NAV: Blood.
JANET: Dripping down titanium poles. White sheets. Starched hard cotton.
NAV: Masses hair masses hair masses scalps heads bodies bolts…

JANET: Bowls bowls bowls.

NAV: Hands cans arms legs. Bolts and batons.

BOTH: It's everywhere.

(*She laughs. They swerve past, in and out of each other. The burst light bulb now creates deeper shadows.*)

JANET: Oh. And… A&E front window? Just been smashed.

NAV (*dodging*): Three bricks.

JANET: Classy. Oh well. Keep calm and carry on. And all that. Isn't it?

NAV: Keep that. Lip up.

JANET: If you've still got it.

BOTH: After this.

JANET: I see the bed coming, rushing down on wheels like some kind of jumbo jet. He looks sixteen or fifteen? Mixed race, maybe? Not sure – I can't tell from here. But his head's slashed and it's bleeding; it's dripping down the wheels and on to the floor, and you can see not footsteps but wheel lines coming down the corridor, and the floor, which is usually alabaster white… not so much. Blood sweeping down it…

NAV: Feels like thirty miles per hour.

JANET: Looks like he's about to take off.

Vroom.

Vroom.

Vroom.

We are ready for take-off!

NAV: OK!

JANET: Right.

BOTH: Keep calm. Keep calm!

NAV: This is not a game. You're real. You're real.

JANET: You've really got the training, you've got the training, the training—

NAV: Oh my—

JANET: I'm going to throw up.

(*Ambulance lights wash over her.*)

NAV: I get information that just bleeps in my ear like an alarm clock that's way too early for your ears but kind of all right for your eyes—

JANET: And I don't understand what the other nurse is saying, but I know that her eyes are telling me to—

NAV: Keep calm!

JANET: Jan, you've never dealt with this much blood before in your entire life.

(NAV *is now thrown into the full action of the riot.*)

NAV: He's crying, screaming.

JANET: He's screaming for his mother.

NAV: He's screaming for his brother.

JANET: He's screaming

NAV: Don't let me die!

JANET: I don't want to die.

(*Pause.* NAV *stands breathless, frozen.* JANET *looks around for someone – anyone.*)

And I look down and… white noise.
NAV: Nothing. Silence.
JANET: I'm told to… and I can't.

(*The ambulance sirens scream louder. As she acts putting pressure on her patient's chest, the sirens morph into lion roars. Vicious. A hunt in the offing.*)

NAV: Hard.
JANET: Sweaty.
NAV: Sticky.
JANET: Hot.
BOTH: I know what this is.
JANET: I put both hands on. As I was trained.
NAV: As I was trained.
JANET: Remember.
NAV: Remember what you're here for.
JANET: Remember… please, just please to God, *please* don't let this be my first. God, he looks like my first boyfriend.
NAV: Oh God.
JANET: Oh God.
Left over right.
One.
Two.
Three.
Hold.

NAV: And, in that moment, I realise… I can't…

(*Pause.*)

JANET: People have moved on. They've moved on to the
next boy… because there's—
NAV: Fifty more coming down the jumbo jet trolley.
JANET: Reeling down their own blood lines. Like a sick
snow day with sledge tracks. And—
NAV: I'm standing there, standing over this fifteen-year-
old…
JANET: He's only about five years younger than me.

(*Pause.*)

Riot in the—
NAV: Moss.
JANET: Borough's burning.
NAV: Basic stuff, they say.
JANET: It's not all in London, eh?
NAV: And I'm alone. Like him. And I stare at him. Like
he is at me.
JANET: And I don't want to leave him alone.
NAV: I don't want to leave him alone.
JANET: No matter how hard I try to move my feet to the
next poor bugger who comes through the doors…
I can't let him go.

(*She breathes harder. He pants. Her hands shake hard.*)

I didn't even know his name.

NAV: And he was screaming. So hard.

JANET: And I know he's gone, but I grab his hand. I see it lying there, sticky. Yellowed fingernails. Smoker. I hold it.

NAV: And I see it.

JANET: I don't know what compelled me to do this – I knew he were dead already. But I just said…

BOTH: I'm here.

JANET: And, I know he didn't squeeze my hand. But it felt like I was, um, I don't know, present for something?

NAV: I was his family—

JANET: In that moment. And I keep holding it. Blood.

NAV: His blood.

JANET: My blood. Someone else's blood. A stranger's blood.

NAV: His body were in front of me.

JANET: And there was this perfect silence.

BOTH: Perfect… almost.

NAV: There was a silence in my head for—

BOTH: The first time—

JANET: During that shift.

NAV: And…

(*They inhale together – a long, hard, painful, smoky breath. Slight pause.*)

JANET: Then this… squeal came out of his mouth.

(*They exhale together – a rasping wheeze.*)

NAV: I didn't know what to do.

JANET: It gave me the shits, man.

> He…
>
> Were…

NAV: He did…

JANET: His…

NAV: Last…

JANET: Breath.

> And his back arched as he vommed out the last bit of air from his lungs. Like a squeal…
>
> Like a—

NAV (*slowly*): —pig.

JANET: And then his arched back flattened back down.

NAV: His head went back to exactly the way it was.

JANET: You sort of get that second chin when you're like that, don't you?

(*Pause.*)

> We ain't got the space. We ain't got the space for these boys—

NAV: And yet, there's plenty more where they came from.

JANET: What am I going to do?

NAV: I was supposed to—

JANET: Save him and—

NAV: And I'm sorry.

JANET: I'm so…

> So…
>
> Sorry.

BOTH: I didn't mean to kill him.

(*She wipes her forehead and he readjusts his belt. She re-enacts the A&E scene around* NAV, *who is frozen with shock on the streets. He stands motionless, as if time has stopped and he is trapped in that moment.* JANET *rushes to various patients across the stage. The space is moving, warping, tilting with radio crackles. Police lights flash. The sound of ECG machines thump.* NAV *stands motionless, as if he is about to be sick. An alarm screeches.*)

JANET: We weren't allowed to have a side.
NAV: We weren't allowed to have a political opinion.
BOTH: What have I done?

(*The sound of the ECG machine thumps underneath. They are catatonic, robotic, almost, in their exhaustion.*)

NAV: My head is spinning, and not in a—
JANET: I'm on a really drunk night out—
NAV: I want chips kind of way.
BOTH: I don't know if I can go back.

(*Silence.* JANET *lights a cigarette. She inhales deeply on it. She offers it to him. He thinks, takes it and drags on it. He coughs. She smirks, but he doesn't. Pause. He leans towards her.*)

NAV: His name was Ryan. He had two brothers. He was in his second year of cookery school. Apprenticeship.

(*Pause. The ECG thump picks up again. Lights dart back and forth, back and forth. Eventually* NAV *and* JANET *return to the present again.*)

BOTH: That's what happened.
NAV: I did it.
     I killed him.
JANET (*laughing*): No, did you ever.
NAV: But I did.
     You know I did.
     Come on.
     So, why haven't you screamed for help yet?

(*She stops and looks at him hard.*)

ACT THREE

Continued.

JANET (*still laughing*): Like you did! Of course you did! Constable Gupta, I know you didn't. Because I did. I know you keep saying I didn't, but I did. I was responsible for his life in that ward – it's my job. We get told we're going to kill someone eventually. Everybody does. That's what you said, right? And that was mine tonight. I must live with that. You should really arrest me. I mean, I'm not going to ask you to. You're not, are you?

(*Pause.*)

Besides, you're just… not the type… You're just not.

(NAV *looks at her hard.*)

Tell me you're not. I'm the type of person – me, not you.

NAV: I did.

(*Silence.*)

JANET: Ryan, Ryan, Ryan. You keep saying his name. Over and over. Why? Why?!

NAV: Because I already knew him. And now he's dead because of me.

JANET: Nav, what did you do?

(*He moves around the room.* JANET *keeps her distance from him.*)

NAV: I'm usually very good at telling the truth. This isn't me. I'm really good at telling the truth, but… it's… you've made it so hard. And I feel like the pig you think I am. But that's what we've got. We have this, here, now and right now. I need to tell you that. Ryan lying on your ward, on your bed, the blood that is dripping into your sink right now, into the dirty tea mugs, is Ryan's. Because I did it. I wanted to tell you before, but… He knew me. He ran to me because he thought I was safe. Because he thought he'd be safe with me. I was the one who was going to make everything better. And I didn't.

(*She moves over to the door.*)

Just stay there!

(*He puts his arm out to stop her.*)

I will not let anyone else die on my watch tonight!

JANET: Tonight?

(*Silence.* JANET *stares at him in a different light.*)

    I should check your uniform… See if the toothpaste
    worked.

NAV: It happened so fast. So fast. It was an accident and—

JANET: You wanted to see if I'd worked it out yet? Is that
    why you're here?

NAV: No, I… liked you… and I didn't want you to think
    it was you.

JANET: People are treating it as just a casualty of the riot.
    But it's not!

NAV: I need you to help me, Janet.

(*They stand facing each other. Silence.*)

JANET: You should go. Now.

(*Pause.*)

    What are you waiting for? Now!

NAV: Janet, please. I'm not leaving you like this, after
    what's happened between us.

JANET: Nothing has happened between us! Nothing.
    OK? Something happened to *you*! Not me.

NAV: Janet, please, I'm trying to tell you—

JANET: You've told me enough for me to know what's
    going on here.

NAV: I didn't mean to hurt—

JANET: Oh, your kind never does.

NAV: My kind?

JANET: You know what I mean.

NAV: You don't mean this, any of this.

JANET: Just like you didn't mean to kill Ryan tonight?!

NAV: Don't shout.

JANET: I have every right to shout when there's a murderer in my flat!

NAV: I'm not a—

JANET: You're not? Then what do I call you?

NAV: It was me, yes. I've said it now. But don't you feel
better that it wasn't your fault in the hospital, at least?

JANET: Oh, yeah. I feel miles better now.

(*They begin circling, distant from one another.*)

NAV: Janet…

(*Pause.*)

JANET: Nav…

NAV: You're not going to do anything—

JANET: If you even *dare* to say stupid, I swear you'll come
out of this a whole lot worse than I will.

NAV: I don't want to hurt you.

JANET: Oh, you're definitely a killer.

NAV: I didn't want to be. I'm not like that. That's not
what happened.

JANET: Killer freaks always say that! 'I didn't mean it. I'm
sorry. It was an accident.' Blah blah blah.

NAV: Can't you let me finish?

JANET: I should have known from the beginning that I couldn't trust an officer. You killed him. A court's not gonna want to know the details. It's pretty black and white! Either someone's dead because of you, or someone's alive because of you.

NAV: I really wouldn't shout with the rioters so close.

JANET: Afraid of the jackals outside, are you, tiger? Need a cage as bad as I do? Cos that's all they want to do. Lock us both up.

Why not?

WHY NOT?!

HELLO OUT THERE! THERE'S A MURDERER IN HERE WITH ME! HELP ME BEFORE HE…

You know what, I did learn something from that little story of yours: tigers belong in cages.

NAV: Ryan was one of us. One of mine! Do you have any idea what that's like?

JANET: No, I don't. What about his mum? His dad? His grandparents? I wonder if they came as far as yours for a better life for their children. For their grandchildren? And you do this to them!

NAV: Don't lecture me about things you don't even come close to understanding. I've… you've… this is…

JANET: You can brag about your Uganda, your Gulab jamuns, your… tigers! But I know you. All I've known is work – that's what I've always done! I can't run away to another country when it gets hard – I stay here. And yes, it has been hard! It has been hard getting by!

(NAV *stays silent. Hurt. Punctured.*)

Tell me, did a little part of you enjoy killing him? That child? That boy? Did it like killing that Indian part of you? *Constable?*

NAV: I dunno, did that working-class chip on your shoulder you've been carrying disappear with his last breath?

JANET: I...

NAV: Cos you seem to remember a lot of details about his passing. Seems you could have done more...

JANET: We are nothing alike! It is not the same thing.

(*Pause.*)

You've lied to me, you've manipulated me, you've made me think I've killed someone, you've flirted with me...

NAV: And you flirted with me!

JANET: Christ, I did your laundry for you! And you've killed a boy. A Moss Side boy.

NAV: You don't know what you're... it wasn't like that.

JANET: Please explain to me, because I've never killed anyone before. I may be a lot of things, but I'm not that.

NAV: I'm sorry.

JANET: You.

Are.

Not.

The.

Victim.
Here.
NAV: And you'd like to be?
JANET: Well, it's certainly a night to remember, and there's always self-defence to fall back on.
NAV: Janet?

(*Pause. A siren flares in the distance again.*)

Come on.
JANET: This is my home. My city.
NAV: It's my city too.
JANET: Then you police should treat it that way.
NAV: Order. We've got to have it.
JANET: Yeah, cos you're really in control of the situation. How can you be… why couldn't you just work in your dad's shop?
NAV: The same as you – you wanted more.
JANET: It doesn't come by tearing Moss Side apart! I care about this city!
NAV: So do I!
JANET: Then why'd you do it?! You know why this whole riot's happening, right?
NAV: I've been briefed. I know the story.
JANET: So, you know the sus laws?
NAV: Yes.
JANET: Then why be an officer? Why do it?
NAV: I'm not like them!
JANET: But you could have been.
NAV: **DO NOT PATRONISE ME ABOUT DUTY.** In the Moss. We had to start saying no.

JANET: Manchester's better than this. It's better than the sus. And I know what's going on. We've seen it.

NAV: I've never stop-and-searched.

JANET: But you haven't said anything.

NAV: How can I?

JANET: That's great. No, really.

NAV: You watch too much news making us out to be the bad guys in all of this.

JANET: But you are!

NAV: I could drudge up how your father may have crawled out of a nineteenth-century hell mine with typhoid, but I won't.
All for you.
Just like my parents.

(JANET *is silent.*)

I shouldn't have said that.

(*Pause. They stand facing each other, as though ready to fight.*)

JANET: What will you say?

NAV: About what?

JANET: After this?

NAV: After you?

JANET: About Ryan?

NAV: I'll come clean. I'll tell the Serge everything.

JANET: And you're willing to put your career in the force on the line for that?

NAV: It's what's right.

(JANET *laughs. During the following, she distracts him by egging him on while she edges towards the radio.*)

JANET: Will you mean it?

NAV: Yes.

JANET: How do you know they won't just sweep it under the carpet? Lost in the mess of the riots? A dirty accident?

NAV: It's the right thing.

JANET: Mr Oh So Noble.

NAV: Little Miss I'm So Bloody Unique. You're not!

(JANET *reaches the radio. She grabs it. She presses the button desperately.*)

JANET: HELP ME! HE KILLED RYAN! HE KILLED THAT BOY!

NAV: Hey! Stop it! Stop that now!

JANET: No! Please! I'm alone with him on Tabbard Road!

RADIO VOICEOVER: Hello?

JANET: Thank God! Hello! Navtej Gupta is a murderer!

NAV: Don't listen to her, Serge!

(*The radio crackles hard.* NAV *grabs at the radio and tries to turn it off.*)

JANET: Hello? Please! I'M ALONE WITH HIM!

(NAV *throws himself at her. She dodges him and runs to another part of the room.*)

NAV: JANET!
JANET: Shut up!
NAV: But…
JANET: Shut the fuck up!

(NAV *stays where he is.*)

NAV: It's not working.
JANET: You're lying.
NAV: It hasn't for a while.
JANET: I don't believe you.
NAV: I turned it off.

(JANET *brandishes it at him. She tries again. It crackles, fizzes and chokes.*)

JANET: For fuck's sake!

(*She throws it directly in front of her feet.*)

NAV: Now what?
JANET: Get stuffed! You nearly attacked me earlier!
NAV: What? When?
JANET: When you nearly hit me!
NAV: That was… that had…
JANET: You nearly did.
NAV: It's not black and white.
JANET: The police aren't either.

NAV: You don't know everything. (*Pause.*) Hot Pink—
JANET: Shut up.

(*The radio crackles again.*)

RADIO VOICEOVER (*screaming*): Gupta! Last message received. If that nurse is in *any* harm, you'll be held accountable. What's going on in there? Whoever's there, tell me!

(JANET *and* NAV *exchange a look. Pause. They throw themselves at the radio. Wrestling, jostling, fighting, just like an echo of the riot they tried to remedy. The loss of the blown light bulb can be felt. Shadows hit them hard. Sirens blare past in the distance. Suddenly, the window in the door shatters. A brick has broken the glass. It hits the floor hard. Mirroring the fall at the beginning,* JANET *drops to the ground and* NAV *ducks, covering his head. Both fly to the floor, the frosted glass showering over them.* JANET *crawls to the light switch and tries to turn it on. It won't work. She flicks it angrily back and forth. She crawls to* NAV *and finds him on the floor by the door. She turns him over. There is blood seeping from his shoulder. She doesn't move him. The sound of the ECG machine thumps and echoes.*)

JANET: Ohmygod ohmygod ohmygod ohmygod. Please don't let this be my—

(*She stops herself.*)

Nav!

(*Long pause.*)

NAV (*weakly*): You might just get it tonight.

(JANET *slaps him.*)

JANET: If you were still alive, fucking say!
NAV: The glass got in the way.
JANET: I need to report you.
NAV (*coughing*): So go ahead.

(NAV *writhes in pain in on the floor. Shattered glass falls off him, all around. He screams.*)

JANET: Nav?!

(*She runs to the door and stops in the frame. He cries out. She runs back to him.*)

I can let you die right here in my living room. I can do that.

(*He cries out again.*)

Do you want me to do that?

(*Pause.*)

NAV (*quietly*): I deserve it. Like you said.
JANET: I never said you should die for—

(*He coughs harder. The blood stain broadens.* JANET *runs to his uniform jacket. She grabs it. She throws it over him.*)

No. So here's what we're going to do. It's not as bad as you think, but I need to act fast. You listenin'?

(NAV *nods.*)

NAV!

NAV: Is it really bad?

JANET: No.

NAV: You're lying!

JANET: Yes, it's bad.

NAV: I knew it!

JANET: Well, now we both are liars!

(*Pause.* NAV *struggles on the floor next to her.* JANET *holds him.*)

NAV: What do you think he was thinking – you know, during—?

JANET: I don't want to think about it. We need to concentrate on the situation now.

NAV: I can't stop thinking about it. His voice is in my head.

JANET: Well, stop it.

NAV: I can't! He won't stop screaming!

JANET: That's you, not him!

NAV: Can you hear him, Janet?!

(*Short pause.*)

JANET: Yeah, but I made him stop.
NAV: It was my fault.

(*She looks at his wounds. She winces. It's bad.*)

JANET: Well, it doesn't matter any more.
NAV: You didn't do it. (*Pause.*) I'm scared.
JANET: Me too.
NAV: I don't want to die.
JANET: Think of your Serge, eh?
NAV: I don't do this for his fucking approval.
JANET: Then me. Think of me. Or Uganda. Or jamuns
     or something.
NAV: I don't want to die.
JANET: You'll be all right.
NAV: Is that what you told Ryan?
JANET: Yes…
NAV: I'm going to die. Kill me – that's what you want!

(*He screams again in pain.*)

JANET: NO! Now, let me see…
NAV: Ryan borrowed my ELO record, you know that?
     (*Laughing again in pain.*) His mum hated anything on
     Top of the Pops.
JANET: Was Ryan your family?

(*Pause.*)

     Nav!

NAV: He… he… I couldn't stop it. I couldn't stop it…
He wouldn't stop. None of them stopped. And it it
it it it it it it it happened when I thought it could,
and I didn't know where who or what was being
thrown, and all I could see through was someone
else's shield. Someone else's eyes and the Serge and
the snarls.

(*Lions can be heard roaring from both sides.*)

It wasn't like battlefields used to be. It was just our
road. Our corner. I was there last week. My one day
off. And tonight. The jungle. The fire. The burning.
The glass ricocheted off our heads. I just wanted to
be the best. The best for the Serge. For my dad…

JANET: I help people.

NAV: I save people.

JANET: That's right, you save people.

NAV: No, you save people.

JANET: I need you to calm down.

NAV: Don't tell me to calm down! I've a knife in my back!

JANET: It's not a knife, it's my front door!

NAV: It's still in there. I can feel it.

(JANET *presses his legs.*)

JANET: Can you feel that?

NAV: Feel what? I can only feel it in me.

JANET: OK. I need you to be honest in your replies to
what I'm going to ask you.

NAV: We're with shields. In formation. It's getting worse.
It's getting like how Pap described Uganda in '72.
They break through. We've got to act fast. Contain
them. Contain the street. Control the situation.
A whistle of a petrol bomb. In the Moss!

(JANET *presses higher up his legs.*)

JANET: Can you feel that?
NAV: Yes! (*Pause.*) I trip. I've fallen hard on the corner
of the curb. And it all happened so quick, and this
kid, this boy, is screaming, and we lock eyes. We lock
eyes and we know. And there's a glistening of something in his left hand. A small glitter of the wrist.

(JANET *presses his left arm.*)

JANET: Does that hurt?
NAV: No!

(*He cries out.*)

JANET: Nav…
NAV: I block with my right arm; I throw the knife on the
floor.

(JANET *continues to check him.*)

He spits in my face and something inside me…
My fist came out and through the smoky air. Hard.

And… it felt… it felt… But he's still standing, and I hit him again and again, but he gets me. I fall hard, and my hand nudges the blade on the floor. It's coming towards me. It's running at me. I can't… I… but I snatch it in my hand and hold it up.

JANET: What happened? Nav! What happened?

NAV: I push it hard into something soft. And then it gets sticky.

(JANET *runs her hand up his back.*)

JANET: Tell me when it starts hurting.

(*She continues to check him over while he speaks. It clearly hurts. She begins to suspect it might be a fatal wound.*)

NAV: He falls. It's the knife. It's his knife. It's my bruises on him. And I look down and it's Ryan. It's Ryan. From Dad's shop on Sundays. Does cookery school. Always came in for crispy pancakes. And… I… no one notices. I see nothing. Except Ryan. Except Ryan from our street. Our Ryan in the Moss.

(*He cries out in pain.*)

Now!

JANET: There?

NAV: Yes! There!

Then horses came! They came like they always do. I didn't know if he'd survived or not until… you.

(*Something in* JANET *clicks.*)

JANET: Look at me.
Look at me.
I'm not losing you too.

(*Pause.*)

NAV: What's going to happen now? Janet?
JANET: Yes?
NAV: Janet?
JANET: I'm still here.
NAV: I didn't mean to. Oh God.

(*He breaks down.*)

They'll have my badge for this. If this gets out.

(*She takes his hand.*)

JANET: He didn't know who you were.

(*Pause.*)

Nav?
Nav?
Come on, now. I need you to focus.
NAV: I'm going to die, aren't I?
JANET: I'm not going to let that happen.
NAV: You should.

JANET: Stop it.

NAV: I deserve it.

JANET: We… all make mistakes.

(*He yelps again. Pause.* JANET *sees the ornamental lion on the floor, which was knocked there by the brick. She roars weakly as she rushes past it.*)

NAV: You are so… bloody… annoying.

(*He tries to get up.*)

JANET: Stop it.

NAV (*trying to laugh it off*): I am, really.

JANET: You're not. Now, stay still!

(*He tries again.*)

> That's an order! I need to look at it. I'm going to turn you. It might hurt.

(*She twists him slightly.* NAV *cries out.*)

NAV: Stop! Stop!

JANET: Done now.

NAV: Where is it?

JANET: There's some shrapnel in your right shoulder.

NAV: I can feel it.

JANET: I think it's your scapula.

NAV: It feels huge.

JANET: It's good. It means it's not an artery. And it's not
    your left side. You're lucky.
NAV: I'm lucky?!
JANET: Shut up! I'm going to take it out.
NAV: You're what?!
JANET: I think I can do this.
NAV: You think?!
JANET: It needs to come out.
NAV: But—
JANET: It's better that I do.
NAV: No! Don't! I remember first aid and blades – you're
    not supposed to pull them out! I'll bleed out!
JANET: That's blades. This isn't.
NAV: Don't!
JANET: You're not him!
NAV: Janet!
JANET: Stay there.

(*She goes to the bathroom.*)

NAV: Where are you going?!

(*She returns with a panty liner. She rips open the packaging as she
runs back.*)

JANET: Nav?
NAV: I'm still here.
JANET: Nav, what colour's my hair?
NAV: Huh?
JANET: What colour is my hair?!

NAV: Um, pink?

JANET: Wrong.

NAV: Hot pink.

JANET: Right. What do you eat at Diwali? Gulab something, right?

NAV: Gulab jamuns!

JANET: They sounded yummy. What was in them?

NAV: Rose water, pistachios—

JANET: Is anyone waiting for you at home? They'll miss you.

NAV: Hang on, you're doing the questions on me!

(JANET *moves behind him. She puts her hands on his chest.*)

JANET: …you can beat him, you can cheat him… you can—

NAV: —treat him bad!

(*She pulls it out fast, efficiently and throws it across the room.* NAV *cries out.*)

What colour is it?

(*She stretches the panty liner and holds it on the wound.*)

JANET: Light red. Not dark and pulpy.

NAV: Put it back in!

JANET: I can't!

NAV: Try!

JANET: You know I can't do that.

NAV: It feels hot… And sticky. I know what this is.

JANET: You're not Ryan.

NAV: Hard.

Sweaty.

Sticky.

Hot.

BOTH: I know what this is.

JANET: Both hands on. As I was trained.

NAV: As I was trained.

JANET: Remember.

NAV: Remember what you're here for.

JANET: Remember, remember… Please, just please to God, please don't let this be my first.

NAV: I'm yours tonight, eh, Nurse?

JANET: Shut up. You're going to walk away from this.

NAV: Do you think they're going to let me stay on the force after this? Do you really think they'll still want the Paki on the job after this?

(*The radio breaks through. It crackles.*)

RADIO VOICEOVER: Gupta. Constable Gupta. Come in, Gupta. Are you still flaming alive there? The station's still happening here!

(NAV *looks up at the radio. He flinches away from it.*)

Constable?!

(JANET *thinks.*)

JANET: Keep putting pressure on it!

(*She thrusts his left arm on to the pad and holds it down. She runs to the radio. She flicks it on. The ECG machine thumps fade in, slow and hard.*)

Um, hello! Hello? Gupta here… I mean Janet. Yes, *that* nurse. He's here with me. Sorry, I've never done this before.

(*She gestures to* NAV*. Slight pause.*)

Urgent backup required at 56 Tabbard Road. And hurry!

(*Radio cuts out. Silence.* JANET *turns back to* NAV*.*)

Nav?
NAV: Yeah?
JANET: When they come for you, and they'll come, I don't think we should talk about what happened tonight.

(NAV *looks to her.*)

I mean it.

(*Sirens begin distantly. They lean against the wall together. He turns his face from her, looking forward again.*)

Nav?!

(*Pause.*)

NAV?!

NAV (*weakly*): I'm still here, Hot Pink.

JANET: I could still kill you!

NAV (*weaker*): At least wait until we've had that drink. Wish I'd had one now.

JANET: I'm on duty tomorrow. I forgot.

NAV: I'll wait.

JANET: We'll see.

NAV: Keep calm and carry on.

JANET: And all that.

NAV: Isn't it? Keep that lip up.

JANET: If you've still got it, eh?

(*She laughs weakly.* NAV *doesn't answer again.*)

NAV: I don't want to die.

JANET: You're not going to.

(*Silence. Sirens and roars grow in a crescendo while* JANET *and* NAV *wait for the police to arrive. The ECG machine continues to thump. They take each other's hands. The thump of the ECG fades.*)

He can't be my first.

(*She leans against his shoulder. Still. Blackout.*)

ACKNOWLEDGEMENTS

Thank you to Charlotte Everest, Francis Grin and Jennie Eggleton at Mrs C's Collective for your dramaturgical support and trust. I'd also like to personally thank Georgi McKie for her directorial, personal and creative support in Manchester.

Thank you to my Mum, who was a student nurse during the Moss Side riots, to whom I owe inspiration and thanks for her accounts of the events. She'd like to add that this play is not based on her life story.

These acknowledgements can't be considered complete without a nod to Harlem Spirit, whose single 'Dem a Sus (In the Moss)' – a reference to sus law, the stop-and-search laws in effect at the time, widely condemned for allowing for racial profiling – was a huge inspiration, and their words, 'Don't let them pressure us', echo through time.

ALSO BY EMMA ZADOW

Alice hasn't been home for a while – for seven years, in fact. But when her little sister Lo tries to take her own life, she has to return to the life she left behind. The change of scenery from London to Norfolk proves quite the culture shock, however, and Alice has to confront what she left behind all those years ago.

The sisters' relationship hasn't evolved in Alice's absence, and when she steps through the door she's plunged back into the same world she escaped from. Set against Norfolk's bleak landscapes, but masquerading as childhood nostalgia, *Fridge* is an all-too-familiar exploration of the broken promises of youth, and a bitter exposition of a generation left behind.

ISBN: 9781913724238 • 96pp • £10